FRANKENKIDS

Other books in the Nightmare Club series

THE NIGHTMARE CLUB

FRANKENKIDS

BY
ANNIE GRAVES

ILLUSTRATED BY
GLENN McELHINNEY

MINNEAPOLIS

First published in Dublin, Ireland by Little Island
Original edition © Little Island 2012

American edition © 2015 Darby Creek,
a division of Lerner Publishing Group, Inc.

Main body text set in ITC Stone Serif Std. 11.5/15
Typeface provided by Adobe Systems.

Darby Creek
A division of Lerner Publishing Group, Inc.
241 First Avenue North
Minneapolis, MN 55401 USA

For reading levels and more information, look up this title
at www.lernerbooks.com.

Library of Congress Cataloging-in-Publication Data

Graves, Annie.
    Frankenkids / by Annie Graves ; illustrated by Glenn
McElhinney.
        pages   cm. — (The Nightmare Club)
    Originally published: Dublin, Ireland : Little Island,
2012.
        ISBN 978-1-4677-4352-5 (lib.bdg. : alk. paper)
        [1. Scientists—Fiction. 2. Brothers—Fiction. 3.
Monsters—Fiction. 4. Horror stories.] I. McElhinney,
Glenn, illustator. II. Title.
PZ7.G77512Fr 2015
[Fic]—dc23   2014015395

Manufactured in the United States of America
1 – SB – 12/31/14

For all my pets, past and present—
but especially past

Annie Graves is twelve years old, and she has no intention of ever growing up. She is, conveniently, an orphan, and lives at an undisclosed address in the Glasnevin area of Dublin, Ireland, with her pet toad, Much Misunderstood, and a small black kitten, Hugh Shalby Nameless.

You needn't think she goes to school—pah!—or has anything as dull as brothers and sisters or hobbies, but let's just say she keeps a large black cauldron on the stove.

This is not her first book. She has written eight so far, none of which is her first.

Publisher's note: we did to try to take a picture of Annie, but her face just kept fading away. We have sent our camera for investigation but suspect the worst.

THANK you!

Look, this is my book and I wrote it, even if the mysterious stranger was the one who told the story. Other people do tell the stories, but I'm the one who writes them down, because I'm the author, and that's what I'm good at—*very* good at, actually.

But I'd better say thanks to my delightful editors at Little Island. And those nice Arts Council people and all. And whoever makes the tea. And the pictures. (They're good, I have to say. Even the one of me.)

And thank you for buying my book. You are clearly a person of exquisite taste.

OK, you know how it goes. My house. My friends. Sleepover. Everyone tells a story—and it'd better be scary!

So this night, after someone had told a pretty spooky story (I thought) and we were all just recovering, this sneering voice comes from a corner.

"Call that a scary story?"

I *love* a good dramatic entrance.

Even *I* jumped a little as a tall boy stepped out of the shadows.

A *strange* tall boy. His skin was pale, marble white, making his yellow eyes and dark red lips stand out. I had to look away. And his voice. His voice...

"That wouldn't scare pimples off my aunt Petunia," he said, smirking.

We made room for the mysterious stranger in the circle of the Nightmare Club, and he started to tell his story.

"You know Frankenstein wasn't the monster?" he said. We all sighed at the same time. (We *knew* that.)

"Frankenstein was the mad scientist who made the monster. He's the really scary one. *Doctor* Frankenstein."

We settled ourselves down and listened. And this is the story the strange boy told...

f course, *Frankenstein* is an old story that's been told to death. Movies. Books. Games. Mash-ups. Costumes. Cereal boxes. Music videos.

It's all fake anyway, right? But it was enough to get my uncle to try his hand at this Frankensteining business.

See, Uncle Fraser
was lonely. He
was old. He had
no one to leave
his money to. And
he lived in a big,
old, falling-over-all-
by-itself house, away
from everyone else.

If he hadn't become a mad scientist on his
own, people would have invented stories
about him anyway.

But that's what he did. He went mad and
tried to build himself...a *friend.*

I didn't know Uncle Fraser. My family wanted nothing to do with him after that time he tried to chew the tail off our dog, Mr. Snookles.

All I have as proof are the stories I've heard. The eyewitness accounts, the newspaper cuttings, and the tales whispered by kids on playgrounds.

Uncle Fraser started small, they say. (It's what you do, scientifically speaking, when you're becoming a mad scientist. You start small.)

First you draw plans on paper napkins and roam the streets talking to yourself, smelling like you haven't had a bath in years.

Then you start telling passersby.

You might yell at an old lady at a bus stop. Or shake a kid outside a corner shop.

It builds your reputation. Word travels fast, and once the world thinks you're a mad scientist, well, the rest is easy.

Uncle Fraser locked himself into his big house as soon as the complaints started.

First it was the town officials asking him to leave the old ladies at bus stops alone.

Then parents worried that shaking their precious children would dislodge a brain cell.

And when the police started asking if he knew anything about dead family pets being dug up from their graves, it was time for Uncle Fraser to retire from public life.

By now Uncle Fraser had collected a
freezer full of dead family pets:

Dogs.
Cats.
Hamsters.
Canaries.
Snakes.
Rabbits.
Parrots.
Weasels.
Tortoises.
Even a monkey.

If I had to guess, the most fun part would be putting things together, inventing the combinations.

Brain of a tortoise.

Body of a hamster.

Hind legs of a small dog.

Front legs of a monkey.

Maybe the tail of a snake.

AAAAAAGH

Trial and error would be the best way.

Then there'd be all that cutting through flesh and sewing sinews. Cobbling muscle and bone together into working order.

At first, nobody noticed anything.

Then the town energy board began to record odd spikes in electricity.

The police got reports of break-ins where the criminal hadn't stolen anything, but extension cables had been left plugged in.

Of course it was
Uncle Fraser trying
to zap life into his
canary-cat-monkey-tortoise.

Or his tortoise-hamster-dog-monkey-
snake.

Or his spider-parrot-weasel-rabbit.

And that needed far more electricity than
Uncle Fraser had in his own house.

Thanks to those trusty extension cables
with their mega-amount of electricity,
and an *awful* lot of luck, Uncle Fraser
managed it.

ZZZAP!!

Pamela was his first success.

Part parrot, part cat, part monkey.

The electricity coursed through Pamela's
body, with different parts springing to life
faster than others.

Unknown to Uncle Fraser, that night was Halloween.

It was a local Halloween tradition for kids to dare each other to visit the huge house with the crazy old man in it.

And this Halloween was no exception.

As Uncle Fraser spewed electricity into the half-cat, half-monkey with parrot wings, the Landy brothers were creeping up the drive to the house.

They jumped every time a flash lit up the overgrown garden around them.

And then they laughed.

And then they crept a little closer.

The older brother, Derek, punched his younger brother's arm and called him a nerd.

"Shut up," said Jake, the younger brother, moving closer to the house. He was clearly the braver of the two.

"Maybe this isn't such a good idea," Derek whispered, crouching behind Jake.

Another
white flash
lit up the garden
as Jake turned to face his older brother.

He could see how scared Derek was, and
that made him braver.

Older brothers aren't supposed to be
frightened easily. Derek was a wuss.
He was worse than a wuss—he was a
total wimp.

Just as Jake was about to say, "Maybe you're right, let's get out of here," Pamela erupted into life inside the house.

The boys fell silent as the sound of flapping, crashing, shouting, and meowing became louder and louder.

Inside the house, Uncle Fraser was laughing like a maniac as Pamela's parrot parts started to flap, sending feathers in all directions.

Then the monkey tail started to swing.

And the cat legs began to kick.

Finally, the rest of Pamela's body, made up of a local tomcat, kicked into life, bouncing around Uncle Fraser's living room / laboratory.

Pamela toppled bottles and overturned
tables as it jumped and flapped and
half-flew, meowing and hissing, around
the room.

Uncle Fraser chased it, calling it to him.

Pamela didn't stop.

It flap-jumped through the open window.

Of course, you should not knowingly leave a window open while you are trying to bring a dead pet to life. Or bits of several dead pets.

Uncle Fraser knows that now.

Jake and Derek
were still crouching
in the driveway
of Uncle Fraser's
house.

They watched the
cat-monkey-parrot
flap and mewl as it
scuttled up the side
of the house until it
reached the roof.

Uncle Fraser, hanging out the open window, called out, "Pamela! Pamela, come down!"

The boys watched in silence.

"Here, kitty, kitty, kitty," Uncle Fraser went on. "I have a banana!"

Pamela was not interested in bananas.

"Pamela!" Uncle Fraser called again in desperation, waving his arms, before disappearing back inside the house.

Jake turned to Derek, smiling. "Did you see that?"

Derek's face was pale, and his mouth was open. He didn't say anything.

His eyes were fixed on the roof of the house. His eyes, in fact, were fixed on Pamela, who was curled up on the chimney.

"Did you see that?" Jake asked again.

Derek still didn't say anything. Drool was starting to flow from the corners of his mouth.

Jake gave up trying to talk to his older brother and turned back to the house.

He could see Pamela too, its body curled round the chimney pipe, its cat tongue licking the monkey paws on its back legs.

"Awesome," Jake said, skulking closer to the house.

Derek didn't move.

Somewhere between leaving his drooling brother and getting closer to the house, Jake had an idea.

Like many ideas that are hatched on a cold, dark night outside the house of a known mad scientist, it wasn't a very good one.

Jake decided to climb a tree that was just outside Uncle Fraser's house.

At the very top of this tree were branches that reached Uncle Fraser's roof.

And on that roof, as we know, was a chimney. A chimney with a cat-monkey-parrot curled up on it.

Jake climbed fast, racing to reach Pamela
before it jump-flap-climbed away.

I'm not certain that Jake had thought any
of this through.

I doubt he was planning on giving Pamela
back to Uncle Fraser once he had caught it.

I don't imagine he had any idea what
he would feed a parrot-monkey-cat once
he got it home. (Cold minced beef with
peanut butter and chocolate banana mice,
maybe?)

What is certain is that Jake hadn't realized
the house was so old. (That's a nice way of
saying it was falling down.)

Jake reached the top of the tree, shimmied out along the branch, and stepped onto the roof.

Almost instantly, the thick black tiles began to slide out from under his feet, falling and smashing on the drive below.

Jake was in serious danger of falling through the roof.

Or sliding right off, down onto the driveway.

Either way, it was going to hurt.

Jake clambered, scrambled, clawed, and finally pulled his way to the chimney, where Pamela sat licking itself.

"Nice kitty," he said in his most soothing voice.

Pamela batted Jake's hand away as he reached for it.

Next time he reached out, Pamela scratched his hand, to make sure he got the message.

Jake pulled
his hand back with a
howl and lost his footing.

He was scrambling now, his feet
dislodging more tiles as he struggled to
find his balance.

At last Jake got a grip on the concrete
around the chimney, and this time he
didn't hesitate.

He grabbed hold of Pamela and bundled
the cat-monkey-parrot under his free arm.

Pamela meowed, hissed, and twisted until finally its entire body was wriggling free of Jake's grasp.

Its wings flapped furiously, sending feathers into Jake's face.

Its front cat claws scratched, and it hissed and spat and bit with its cat mouth.

The monkey paws clawed and slapped and pulled until Jake couldn't hold on anymore—and Pamela burst free.

Jake lost his footing again.

There was nowhere for him to balance.

He reached out and clung to the chimney,
his body flat against the roof and his legs
kicking behind him.

In the way that old falling-down houses
do, the chimney started to crack and
crumble.

Jake let out a scream for help.

EAM

Uncle Fraser heard it first, the sound traveling down the chimney and into the living room, where he was busy preparing his next experiment.

Of course he went outside to see who was calling. He might be able to help. (He was mad, but he wasn't evil.)

Derek heard Jake's scream too.

His eyes snapped into focus.

He shook his head, slurped the drool back into his mouth, and rushed forward to help his brother.

Three things happened very quickly:

First, the chimney broke free from its perch
on the roof, sending bricks, concrete, and
Jake tumbling down.

Second, Derek reached the front of
the house just as his brother fell, and a
chimney's worth of bricks fell on top of him.

Third, Uncle Fraser opened his front door to
the sight of two brothers stuck under a pile
of roof tiles, bricks, and chimney pieces.

One of the boys had a mangled spine, and his arms were broken.

The other brother's legs were crooked and crushed.

They were both unconscious.

Looking at them, Uncle Fraser had an idea.

The two brothers woke to the same
feeling: a cat licking their toes.

"That tickles!" Derek laughed, turning his
head.

His brother was lying beside him. He was
laughing too.

"Stop!" Jake pleaded between giggles. "Please!"

He kicked his feet.

The licking stopped, and both boys sat up and looked at their feet.

Pamela was crouched at the end of the bed, ready to pounce on their toes.

Derek didn't recognize his legs. Or his toes.

"Jake?" he said, turning to his brother.

Jake turned to face Derek at the same
moment, and their noses touched.

I can't be certain which brother screamed
first or for longest—my sources aren't
entirely reliable—but both boys screamed.

And screamed.

And screamed.

SCREEEEEEEEEAAAAAAAAAAAAAAAMMMMMMMMMWWWWWWWWWW

They went on screaming until Uncle Fraser appeared in the room, holding two cups.

At the sight of Uncle Fraser, their screams got louder, until neither brother could scream anymore.

Uncle Fraser handed them a cup each. Derek reached with his right hand and took one.

Jake tried to use *his* right hand, only to find it already had a cup in it.

Both brothers looked down at their body at the same time, and the screaming began again.

"I'm sorry, boys," Uncle Fraser said, looking at Derek. "I could only save one body. Half of you—"

He looked at Jake.

"And half of *you.*"

"But we're..." Derek started.

"...*attached!*" Jake finished.

"We've been...*Frankensteined,*" Derek squealed.

"You could say that," said Uncle Fraser. "I thought I might call you the Frankenkids."

The two heads on one body began screaming again.

Uncle Fraser lifted Pamela up into his arms and left them to it. "Some people just don't know how to say thank you," he muttered.

THE END

I suppose that's scary,
if you go for that sort
of thing.

More annoying—
I didn't even
get to tell the
mysterious
stranger what I
really thought of his
story. By the time I'd
come out from hiding behind my
hands, he was gone. And so was Kate.

We've never lost a member before.

Now we're *all* screaming.

AAAAAAAARGH!